BLACK HOLE RADIO

BILALUNA

ANN BIRDGENAW

ILLUSTRATIONS BY E.M. ROBERTS

DFP

DartFrog Plus

DartFrog Plus

Publisher Information:
DartFrog Books
4697 Main Street
Manchester Center, VT 05255

www.DartFrogBooks.com

CONTENTS

CHAPTER 1

LIFE IS BUT A DREAM

We're back in 'Mission Control'. I look over to see Matt snoring on the other side of the couch, using his awesome afro for a pillow. *Phew!* I breathe a sigh of relief.

Beep, beep, beep, beep!

"Nooooo, not again!" I cry, jumping over the back of the couch, hiding there. My heart is pounding in my chest.

"Matt!" I hiss, trying to wake him up quietly. "Matt! Wake up!" I whisper louder. Matt comes to, looking groggy and confused.

"Where am I?" he asks looking around.

"Matt . . . I'm back here," I say.

Matt looks over the back of the couch with sleepy eyes, "What are you doing back there?" He scratches his head and rubs his eyes. "Hawk! Did it all really happen?"

I shoot my eyes towards the closed garage door. "I'm not sure, Matt . . . but I just heard beeping coming from the garage."

"No way!" Matt yelps, jumping over the back of the couch. He lands with a thud, fully awake now.

Beep, beep, beep, beep!

"It can't be!" he says, with eyes big as saucers. "We didn't really travel through your haunted garage to another planet, did we?" He looks at me in disbelief.

We gave our rings to Dweezil and Zzznap!!

I crawl out from behind the couch, away from the door leading to the garage.

"I don't know! I thought it was a dream too when I woke up. But how could we both have the same dream?"

Looking down, I realize that I don't have my club ring on my hand anymore and remember that Matt and I gave our rings to Dweezil and Zzznap before we left planetoid Shnergla.

Matt looks at me strangely. "Hawk, did you just say that you remember giving our club rings to Dweezil and Zzznap?" he asks, looking down at his hand.

"No, but I was thinking . . ." *Whaaaaaaaaat! Did Matt just read my mind?*

"Yes," he says, looking at me with wide eyes.

"Okay, Matt," I say urgently. "Think about something right now."

"Uh, okay," he says, putting his hands in his pockets and shifting his feet.

"No, I don't want to know how badly you need to go to the bathroom!" I say, rubbing my head. "This is serious, Matt. I think we can read each other's minds, like Shnerglers! Wait. maybe that's the gift that She-Shnerg gave us before we left." I pace around 'Mission Control', tearing at my tangled, dirty blond hair. "I knew it would be something weird and wonderful . . . but like ESP!"

"But, but . . . that would mean that it's all true and it really did happen," Matt says quietly, as the realization hits us both at the same time.

Beep, beep, beep, beep!

OMG! We ARE the Worm-Ones!

CHAPTER 2

A PLANETOID FAR, FAR AWAY

Before I go any further, I should tell you what happened to Matt and me on the most unbelievable, intergalactic day of our lives.

If you do not believe in black holes, wrinkles in time, wormholes and portals to outer space, you should close this book right now.

Okay, I can continue.

Matt and I were in 'Mission Control', the headquarters for our space club 'Uranus is the Butt of the Solar System'—UBSS for short. We were ready to watch our favorite TV show, *Star Trekkers*, when we heard a beeping sound coming from the garage. At first, we thought the garage was haunted, but it was something much crazier than that! We discovered the beeping was coming from a small transistor radio in a box with my grandpa's old stuff. Before we knew what was happening, we got sucked into an electromagnetic radio force-field and ended up on a small planet far, far away.

I know crazy, right?

. . . well now it's beeping again!

Beep, beep, beep, beep.

"Hawk!" Matt hisses, backing away from the garage door. "What do we do?"

Matt thinks I'm actually a genius like Stephen

Hawking—the famous cosmologist I'm named after.

"C'mon Matt, let's get out of here! It wants to turn us into Worm-Ones again!" I run across the lawn towards my house, and as far away from the radio as possible. "Let's go to my room. It's early and my parents are still sleeping." We slide into the quiet house.

"Wait a sec. How come our parents aren't out searching for us? We must have been missing for days," Matt whispers, as we creep up the stairs and into my room. He looks nervously out the window at our clubhouse before collapsing on my bed.

"No Matt," I say, checking my phone. "It's only Saturday morning."

"Like, where did all the time go?" asks Matt, pulling a pillow under his head, getting comfortable.

I boot up my laptop. "I think it has something to do with Albert Einstein's theory about space-time. Let's look it up online."

"Einstein was a really smart guy who figured out that time slows down as you get close to moving at the speed of light, which is 186,000 miles per second. So, one day traveling through space could be like 50 years in Earth time."

"My head hurts," Matt cries, putting a pillow over his head, "I wanna go to sleep."

"Einstein showed that time moves faster when gravity is lower, and the planet's orbit is slower."

"Stop, Hawk, my brain is going to explode."

MOONSCAPE
FUTURE OF THE SPACE STATION
STRANGE SPECIES
STAR TREKKERS

"It's simple, Matt—we went through a wormhole to get to Planetoid Shnergla and no time passed. But because the gravity and orbit speed of Shnergla are lower than Earth's, time moves faster there than here. Even though it felt like we were on Shnergla for a few days, in Earth time, only a few hours passed. So, it's Saturday morning. We slept in the clubhouse, after being gone a few hours on Friday night."

"All I can say is don't wake me up until Monday morning. I haven't slept in 3 light-days." says Matt, falling instantly asleep as I crash out on the other side of the bed. I ESP: good night She-Shnerg. Good night Mung and Dweezil and Zzz . . .

CHAPTER 3

I DON'T LIKE MONDAYS

Monday morning in Mrs. Bupkiss' class I notice Matt fast asleep, face down on his desk. A few kids snicker and point as Matt starts snoring. *Oh brother*. There's spittle and drool leaking out of his gaping mouth onto his desk. *Eeeew!*

"Matthew Finn," says Mrs. Bupkiss, loudly. You know she's not happy with you when she uses your full name.

"Huh, what?" grunts Matt groggily, looking around yawning.

"Maybe you'd like to join the class and answer this question. Who was the first scientist to say that the sun was the center of the solar system and the other planets revolved around it and not the Earth, as people believed at the time?"

Everyone turns to look at Matt, knowing that he has no idea since he snored through the lesson.

Nervously, Matt looks around at the faces watching him and suddenly he says, "Copernicus?" He shoots a look over at me then looks at Mrs. Bupkiss' surprised face.

"That's . . . um . . . correct, Matt. Now go to the board and write down the names of some of the other scientists that we discussed," she instructs.

E=mc²
Galileo Galilei
Isaac Newton
Albert Einstein

As Matt walks shakily up to the front of the class, he starts reading my thoughts and getting the answers. He not only writes the names of the scientists but what they were famous for, including Einstein's famous equation, $E=mc^2$. Mrs. Bupkiss hadn't even mentioned that in the lesson, but I researched it on the weekend.

Matt turns around smiling and some of the kids in the class start to clap. They thought he was going to fail miserably, but he knew all the answers. He takes a bow, and everybody claps, including Mrs. Bupkiss.

After class, I meet Matt at our lockers. "Thanks for bailing me out, man! I didn't know any of those guys. This ESP stuff is great," he says.

"Well, that was an accident. I didn't mean to cheat. It just sort of happened, as I thought of the answers," I tell him truthfully. "We better learn how to control this ESP thing or we're going to know everything about each other."

Just then Matt is swarmed by some classmates asking how he saved himself and knew all the answers. Matt just shrugs. "That was way cool!" someone shouts as Matt gets swept along, down the hall and into the cafeteria. Suddenly, Matt's very popular.

As I watch them head down the hallway, I notice the new girl, Celeste. She's a pretty girl with long red hair, but she looks nervous. She's standing awkwardly by the lockers, trying to stay out of the way. Mrs. Bupkiss said we'd have a new girl joining our class and that she's a little different. I don't know what Asperger's is, but I think that's what she has. Mrs. Bupkiss said she may be shy and doesn't like to make eye contact. What's so different about that? Maybe she's just a little geeky like me. It's not easy to switch schools halfway through the year. Some of the kids think she's weird, but I think she's interesting and I like her red hair. Matt says we're not supposed to like girls yet, but she is one girl I want to know better. I can read Matt's thoughts, but right now I wonder what Celeste is thinking. I hope she doesn't think *I'm* too geeky. *Celestial Celeste*, I think, as I am swept down the hall towards the cafeteria with the rest of the hungry mob.

CHAPTER 4

CELESTE TAKES OVER THE STORY

Hi, I'm Celeste, the new girl Hawk has been talking about. And I'm going to tell the story from here on. I'm very grateful to Hawk for sharing my story. But you know what? When you have Asperger's, your life is filled with two kinds of people—people who think you're weird and make fun of you, and people who want to tell your story. They think they can make other people understand you, and make people nicer to you. But I get tired of people always wanting to tell my story. So, I'm taking over *my* story because I thought you'd like to hear it from me.

I think about how mad I am at my parents right now and rub the worry stone that's in my pocket as hard as I can. At least they gave me a good name—Celeste. Too bad they're both workaholic astronomers. It's always "this star this" and "that planet that", and "did you hear they discovered a new supernova?" What the heck is a supernova anyway? *Rub-Rub*, I wish they would leave the universe alone and spend more time with me. To make things worse, we had to move because mom and dad got new jobs at the university with the best telescope around. Who cares about telescopes? *Rub-Rub.* I had to change schools and leave my one friend behind. They know I hate change. They know I have trouble making friends. All the kids here hate me or avoid me because they think I'm weird. At least I have my ant farm and bug books to keep me busy or I think I'd go crazy. *Rub-Rub-Rub.*

To get away from everyone, I walk over to the edge of the playground.

"Hey you, new girl." a big, stocky kid pulls me out of my thoughts. "I need to explain the rules around here," he says.

"Rules, what rules?" I usually like rules. I'm the queen of rules. But this kid doesn't seem friendly. I take a few steps back.

"Rules about me needing your money so I can buy cookies," he explains with a smile-snarl.

"Listen, Mikey, is that your name? I don't have any money, okay," I respond, not making eye contact and trying to stay cool.

Then the boy named Hawk comes over.

"Hey, Mikey, leave her alone," he says firmly. He tilts his head at me. Does that mean I should run away? I'm not sure.

But that's nice of him.

Mikey's head whips around to see who the suicidal person behind him is. "Oh, it's the Nerd-Bird. Did you give me *YOUR* quarter yet, Hawk?" he says with a sly smile.

Mikey looks away from me and focuses on Hawk. I back away and hide behind a nearby tree, where I can still listen to how this goes down.

"No, and I'm not going to either! You're trying to tax us, and it's not right." Hawk says forcefully.

Big Mikey grabs Hawk's shirt collar and lifts him onto his tiptoes. That's when the sleepy boy Matt, rushes over with a group of kids behind him.

Matt smiles nervously. "Whoa! Mikey, what are you doing to my friend Hawk, here?"

"Stay out of this, Rug -head. You may have impressed those idiots in class, but I know you better than that!" Mikey snarls, pulling Hawk's collar tighter.

Hawk tugs at his collar. "Mikey, (cough) don't you know that Matt has a super-power? Be careful because he knows things about you that no one else knows."

Mikey shoots him a sideways 'Yeah, right!' look.

"No, really! Ask him anything, he knows it," Hawk says, sending Matt a knowing look. "Just whisper it in my ear so I know it's true," Hawk says to Mikey, who seems caught off guard with this turn of events.

"Okay wise-guy, when's my birthday?" Mikey asks, leaning over to whisper the answer in Hawk's ear.

Matt closes his eyes and puts his fingers on his temples like he's focusing his psychic power.

His eyes pop open. "March 15th," says Matt with a grin.

"Wait, that's . . . a . . . a lucky guess!" says Big Mikey, looking around as everybody starts talking excitedly at once. "That was too easy. Answer this," he says, looking less and less sure of himself. "What pet do I have?" Mikey asks Matt and whispers in Hawk's ear.

Matt closes his eyes and rubs his forehead like he's concentrating. "A goldfish named Fred," he answers, opening his eyes.

Big Mikey's eyes go wide in astonishment. "But, but I just got him yesterday, no-no-nobody knows about him," he stammers, as the kids around us all look stunned.

"I told you. Matt can read minds. It's his super-power," Hawk says to a defeated-looking Mikey.

"No way! One more question!" Big Mikey shouts angrily.

"Okay, one more question. But if he gets it right, you have to agree not to bully anyone else, or tax us for our lunch money," Hawk says looking Big Mikey in the eye.

"Okay, okay. Deal! If you can answer this question, I won't bully anyone anymore," Big Mikey says with a sly grin. "What are my parents' names? And I'm not telling anyone the answer," he adds, rubbing his hands together.

Hawk and Matt look nervously at each other.

Matt does his thing, closing his eyes, rubbing his temples like a real psychic. After a few seconds, he says, "Your Mother's name is Gloria, but everyone calls her Goody. And . . . and . . . you . . . don't . . . have . . . a father. You never knew who he was."

Matt's eyes pop open in surprise at what he just said. A hush descends over the crowd as everyone looks from Matt to Mikey and back again.

Shock and anger flash across Big Mikey's face. he yells, "How did you . . . you can't know that! I do so have a father! I do so!" He starts to cry and runs off the playground and into the school.

"Okay everybody, nothing to see here," Hawk says

as all the kids lift Matt over their heads and crowd-surf him into the school, laughing and cheering.

Hawk stays behind and walks towards my hiding spot.

CHAPTER 5

A STAR BY ANY OTHER NAME

"**C**eleste," Hawk calls, as I poke my head out from behind the tree.

I tuck a long strand of my red hair behind my ear. "Thanks for helping me out." *This is so awkward!*

"No problem. I'm Hawk," he says, walking toward me with his hands deep in his pockets.

"I'm Celeste. Ummm, I guess you already know that," I say, blushing and looking away. *What a stupid thing to say! Rub-Rub.*

"Yes. It's a great name. Do you know what it means?" he asks.

"It has something to do with outer space—stars and planets or something. My parents are astronomers. 'Space-Geeks'," I add, making air quotations with my fingers as we walk back to school.

"Cool!" he exclaims. "You're so lucky. It must be great to live with two space scientists!"

I look at him strangely. "Yah, I guess so. But some-times I wish they'd spend more time with me here on planet Earth." I look away before we can make eye contact. I'm not used to talking to boys.

"My Grandpa wasn't a scientist, but he knew all about space and he taught me some. I know all the constellations and the best times of the year to look for shooting stars," Hawk says.

"I love shooting stars, and my favorite constellation is Andromeda," I say. "My mom told me she's known as the 'Lady of the Heavens' and she has red hair like mine." I wonder if I'm talking too much. Mom told me to let others do the talking sometimes. "What's your favorite?" I ask him, as we get closer to school.

"My favorite is Perseus. He has a cool sword he uses to cut off the heads of monsters. I think he saved Andromeda from the sea monster Cetus," Hawk replies.

Cool, he likes Greek Mythology too.

"Their constellations are side by side, and I read in Greek mythology that they got married." *Gulp! What did I just say?* I feel my face burning as it turns red like my hair.

He pretends not to notice, but I feel weird now.

"I like Andromeda too . . ." Hawk says. The conversation trails off as we reach the doors of the school. "Don't worry, Celeste. You'll make lots of new friends here. And Big Mikey won't bother you anymore," Hawk says as he opens the door for me.

"Yah, what happened there with Mikey? How did you and Matt do it?" I ask, looking down at my feet.

"Matt and I learned a thing or two about how to handle bullies. It's a long story." Hawk glances at me then blurts, "Ummm, my Grandpa helped me make an outer space clubhouse next to my dad's garage. Do you want to come over after school and see it?"

Wait, did a boy just ask me over to his house? I'm so flustered right now—this is all happening too fast. But Hawk stood up for me today—and I do want to make some new friends. He seems nice and maybe even as brave as Perseus. Uggh. Why do I have to overthink everything? *Rub-Rub.*

"Ahhh, I don't know . . . I usually go to the library after school, and then my parents pick me up. Ummm, I'll phone them after school to see if it's okay," I say, hurrying into the classroom, looking at the ground. I make my way to the front row where Mrs. Bupkiss assigned me a seat. I turn my head to take a peek at Hawk as he saunters to the back of the class. A wide grin spreads across my face as I think, *Hawk, that's a cool name too. I wonder what it means, a boy called 'Hawk'.*

CHAPTER 6

WELCOME TO THE CLUB

Why did I agree to this? He's not going to like me. Maybe I'll tell him to forget it. I should go to the library like usual. I see Hawk waiting in front of the school with his psychic friend, Matt. I hope he can't read my mind! *Rub-Rub*. Okay, this is good—there'll be three of us. Rubbing my stone for self-confidence, I keep approaching. As I get closer, I overhear bits of their conversation. I have super sensitive ears, but sometimes it can be too much and turns into sensory overload. It's part of my disorder. I used to have to put earplugs in my ears just to go into the schoolyard. But sometimes it helps me to judge the situation . . . like now.

"*Who's* coming to the clubhouse?" Matt asks Hawk in amazement.

"Celeste, the new girl," Hawk answers casually, like it's no big deal. "She's kind of into space too," Hawk adds quickly, as he spots me walking towards them. "Shhh, here she comes," he whispers to Matt. "Act natural."

Matt smooths down his awesome afro. "Okay, okay. I just didn't know we were letting *girls* into the club now."

"Hey, Celeste! You know Matt. He's a member of the club too," Hawk says, looking back and forth between us awkwardly.

"Hi. My parents said I could come over for two hours, and then they'll pick me up at 5:15," I say, rolling my eyes. "Can I text them your address?" I pull out my phone.

"Sure, let's go to 'Mission Control,'" Hawk says, his ears turning red.

Walking into the clubhouse, Hawk seems embarrassed or nervous showing me around. He's talking really fast and tidying up at the same time. There's tacky old furniture, fake knobs, stars and ripped posters of planets on the walls—but it's kind of great.

"Uhhh, it just needs a little fixing up," Hawk says, pushing a mountain of space magazines and Star *Trekkers* comics off of the orange couch so I can sit down.

"No. This is cool! My parents would be very impressed. This is your own space for 'space.'" I say, looking around, and twirling my worry stone furiously.

Hawk and Matt look at each other, crack up and do a high-five. I meant it literally, but I guess they thought it was a joke.

Hawk and Matt do some kind of secret handshake. It makes me feel good when they offer to teach it to me, but I'm not comfortable with touching hands. I close my eyes as we link fingers, do an interlocked fist pump, and then bump knuckles together.

Hawk looks at Matt who nods, "Um, Celeste, do you want to join the UBSS space club?"

"Yah you have to join the club now, Celeste! You know the secret handshake *and* the location of 'Mission Control,'" Matt says, trying to convince me.

I think he liked my joke.

"Okay. Since I haven't had any other offers . . . I guess I'm in," I say, happy that I haven't said anything too weird. "What do I have to do to join?" I briefly wonder if I should ask my parents first. Nah my parents will die of happiness when I tell them.

"Nothing really, just say our 'Uranus is the Butt of the Solar System' pledge of allegiance . . . and maybe order an NSA ring from the back of '*Spaced Out!*' magazine," Hawk stammers. "Ahhh, the rings really work."

I raise my eyebrows, but I don't say anything. They want me to join their club, but I'm nervous. Maybe they'll think I'm weird when they get to know me better.

"Where is that pledge we wrote, Matt?" Hawk says, opening drawers, "Okay, here it is. Put your right hand on your heart and say after me, 'I pledge allegiance to the UBSS Space club, to all space club members and to Planet Earth on which it stands. Many constellations and many galaxies are waiting to be discovered.'"

I repeat it solemnly and seriously. I even like the funny name of the club.

Hawk announces, "You are now an official member of the UBSS Space club." We do our club handshake again.

"Okay now what?" I ask, wandering around 'Mission Control', picking things up and putting them down again. I approach the garage door. "What's in there?"

"NO! Don't go in there!" Matt screams, running over to block the door.

"C'mon, what's in there?" I ask again, getting more curious.

Hawk blurts, "Nothing! There's nothing in there that . . ."

Beep, beep, beep, beep.

"What's that beeping sound?" I ask. The beeping is low, but crystal clear to my ears.

"What beeping sound? I didn't hear any beeping. Did you hear a beeping sound, Matt?" Hawk asks him with his eyes wide.

"Nope, I didn't hear anythi . . ."

Beep, beep, beep, beep.

"How about that?" I ask, cocking my head at them, knowing that they heard it.

Hawk and Matt look at each other, then at me.

"Okay," Hawk declares. "You're a member of our club now, so we can tell you about . . . the wormhole radio that's in my garage."

CHAPTER 7

WORMHOLE WHAT?

I look at them in disbelief. Did I miss an important cue in the conversation like I sometimes do? Is this a joke that I don't get? Then something dawns on me, "Is this a club test, some kind of club-ritual thing where I have to prove myself worthy of being a member?" I ask, reaching for the doorknob.

"No, of course not. We wouldn't do anything like that!" Matt says, shaking his afro violently.

"This is serious, Celeste. We got sucked into it last Friday and . . . well, it's a crazy story, but we barely made it back alive!" Hawk says in all seriousness, while Matt nods and looks like he's about to freak out.

"Come on, you two. You expect me to believe that there is a portal to outer space in your garage?" I ask, going back over the conversation in my mind to see what I missed. At the same time, I try to remember what my parents told me about wormholes. I remember my dad once said: "Think of a wormhole as a tunnel through space. Things can enter the hole at one end and come out the other end in a different part of the universe, millions or even billions of miles away."

"Yes. That's it exactly. It's a portal. And we have to stay away from it," Hawk says, like he's trying to avoid a panic attack, breathing in through his nose, out through his mouth, with his hands on his tousled blond hair.

I think maybe Hawk's got Asperger's too, or he's really agitated about this.

Beep, beep, beep, beep. The sound is louder and more insistent now. It's getting so loud, I wonder if I am going to lose control, what my mom calls getting 'overwhelmed'.

"What are you hiding in there? Is it a secret? I'm good at keeping secrets. I pledged allegiance, remember?" I blurt out, getting panicky. Walking over to the couch, I try to find my focus. *Rub-Rub on my stone.*

Hawk and Matt follow me and Hawk tries to explain, "It's not that we don't trust you, it's just this thing is dangerous, and if we . . ."

My instincts take over and I make a sharp U-turn and run back to the garage door. "I just need to stop that beeping noise," I say over my shoulder as I open the door and run into the garage.

Beep, beep, beep, beep! The sound is much louder and clearer now that the door is open.

"Celeste! Don't do it!" Hawk shouts, as he and Matt jump up and follow me into the garage.

I'm holding the beeping radio out to them as its glowing greenish-yellow light shines in my face. I can't tear my eyes away from it! I am transfixed by the glow and I may be having a cosmic conniption. I don't like this! *What is happening?*

"Matt, you knock the radio out of her hand, and I'll pull her out of here," Hawk yells as they rush across the garage to my rescue.

A static sound is coming from the radio now and it's getting louder. There are crackling and popping noises as a strong electromagnetic field draws me in. Boxes around us shake, rattle and tip over as the overhead light flickers. I'm in full sensory overload mode now, afraid of what is about to happen, but I can't move or speak. I hum a lullaby to myself the way my mom used to calm me down when I was little. Matt tries to grab the radio and he gets locked onto it. Hawk grabs my arm as we are drawn into the glow of the force-field. I can't even reject the physical touching. I'm so shocked right now.

"Noooooo!" I hear someone yell, maybe it's me, or maybe it's all three of us. We spin like tops in zero gravity through a tunnel that seems to stretch and shrink, tilt and straighten as cool flames snake by us at light-speed. Then everything goes dark.

CHAPTER 8

PLANET OF THE BUGS

come to on a rough, charred-black rock. Looking around groggily, either I'm dreaming, or we've landed on the moon! Although it's night, the sky is bright with stars, and I can see all around me. It's a dusty, rocky, barren terrain. But where are Hawk and Matt? I try to get up to look for them and find myself almost floating above the ground. My feet are moving, but I'm not going anywhere. "Whoa!" I yell in surprise, trying to get my footing, I bounce along as I try to walk.

The gravitational field is not very strong here, so I have a hard time keeping my feet on the ground. I look around at the darkness stretching out all around me. *Where am I?* All I see are huge black craters and rolling hills of rock-like lava cooled in its tracks. *I guess Hawk and Matt weren't kidding about the wormhole radio,* I think guiltily. I have to learn to control myself.

"Hawk, Matt!" I call, but the atmosphere is so thin I have a hard time breathing, let alone calling out. There are no plants or trees around, so I guess there's less oxygen in the air. I fall and start to crawl on my hands and knees over the rocky terrain, struggling to breathe. This is all so overwhelming. *What am I going to do? Where am I!*

"Hawk! Matt!" I gasp. "Where" *pant* "are" *pant* "you?" I collapse face down in a crater, exhausted.

Unable to drag myself out of the crater, I roll over onto my back and stare up at the night sky. There are no lights around to cause any light pollution, so I see millions and trillions of stars. I look for my Andromeda and the brave Perseus, but soon realize that I won't see Earth constellations here. This is a strange and new solar system. I shake my head and try to orient myself. There's a misty haze in space, that makes the stars twinkle and change color like they're reflecting off each other. The stars seem to make a big spiraling cone shape, fanning out into the universe. I focus on the sky to calm myself down. I am amazed to see meteors streaking across the sky. *Wow! So cool!* I don't recognize any of the constellations, but I see my favorite 'falling stars'.

"Guys, are you seeing this?" I whisper, gasp, then smile. I try to count the meteors as they streak across the sky overhead, to help me focus, but there are too many. It's a meteor shower! I remember going with my parents up to the large telescope they use out in the wilderness to study the galaxy. One time when they were working for hours on their research, I went outside, lay on the grass and fell asleep. My father rushed around in the dark in a panic looking for me. He didn't get angry when he found me. He just laid down next to me and we looked at the *Milky Way* together.

My parents are always so busy with work, but I love all the 'space' things my mom and dad share with me. I just complain about it sometimes. And I love Greek mythology and all the stories about how the gods are made into constellations when they die. Most kids are not into bugs and constellations like me, but at least my parents understand me. I remember thinking how strange it was when Dad told me that we were looking at history, right there up in the sky. "Honey, we're looking back in time. The light we see now may have taken millions, or billions of years to reach our eyes." *Does that mean I am a million light-years from home?* I love my parents and I worry that I'll never see them again. If I ever get home, I promise I'll never be angry at them again. I feel tears burn my eyes and the sky gets blurry as I wonder if I will ever see my parents, or Hawk and Matt again?

I hear a sound above me. I look up to see four aliens standing on the edge of the crater with weapons drawn and pointing down at me. They look like the aliens in the movie I begged my dad to watch with me, *Planet of the Bugs*!

"Oh, no," I murmur as I pass out.

CHAPTER 9

BILALUNA

I wanna go home! I wanna go home! I don't like aliens and wormholes and . . .

"Celeste, wake up!" I hear Hawk say, shaking me. "Celeste!"

"Huh, what?" I wake up and look around at all the eyes on me. There are Hawk, Matt and two aliens with six eyes each. That's too many eyes!

"Can we go home now?" I moan, trying to get up. I don't like this, it's freaking me out!

"It's okay Celeste, they're trying to help us—I think," says Hawk, grabbing my hand and holding it in an attempt to calm me down. He doesn't realize that he's doing just the opposite, since I don't like holding hands with anyone—*especially boys my age!* But I feel a little calmer now that we're all together.

"Yah, we couldn't find you, Celeste! We didn't know what to do," Matt says in a rush. "We fell into a deep crater and couldn't get out until these guys arrived and levitated us out! It was so cool!"

"Uhhh, Matt," says Hawk, "it wasn't cool when you vomited all over the place and on me! They made me wear this, this worm-skin!" I look down to see he's wrapped in a weird alien drape, and I have to smile because it looks like a dress. But he's still pretty cute.

"What? I always get airsick!" says Matt, looking embarrassed.

One of the aliens approaches and I am struck by what I am looking at. The creature is a giant bug—one that I am not familiar with. Obviously, it's as big as my dad! I am wide awake now!

It clicks and grunts, animating to Hawk, who translates: "He said we landed on Bilaluna. Population 1003, now that we're here."

"Where's that?" Matt asks, looking from one to the other, unsure which eyes to make eye contact with.

I can't stop staring at the two-legged, six-armed bug with a big round, hairy belly and antennas that flow behind him like a horse's mane. His head is heart-shaped and partially transparent and shows his pulsating brain. *Ewwww!*

He squeaks and grunts at Matt, who translates: "He says we're on a moon in the Spiral Galaxy, 2.536 million light-years away from planet Earth." Matt's eyes go wide, as he realizes how far from home we are. "Whoa."

I look at Hawk and Matt waiting for them to explain, but they just stare at me blankly.

"Like how do you know what they're saying?" I ask them both. "All I hear are clicks and chirps," I say, still in shock. *What is going on here?*

"Hawk and I can use ESP to understand them," explains Matt, confusing me even more.

I shake my head. *Is he kidding me?* "What are you talking about? ESP isn't a thing," I say, starting to feel like I fell down Alice's rabbit hole to Planet Wonderland.

"When we went through the wormhole last time, the Supreme leader of Shnergla gave Matt and me a gift of ESP or mind-reading. That's how we fooled Big Mikey today at school." Hawk continues, "But I guess we can read aliens' thoughts too." He nods at Matt who is distracted by the alien next to him.

I start to tear up. "This is so . . . so overwhelming." I choke on the words, "I'm sorry I didn't believe you guys when you told me about the portal." To avoid looking at him, I look around, still hoping I am in a weird dream and might wake up. I rub the worry stone in my pocket when something occurs to me. "You can't read my thoughts, can you?" I ask, surprised that we are even having this conversation. I can hardly keep up with my brain myself. Sometimes I think in pictures instead of words, so I hope this blocks them from eavesdropping on my thoughts.

"No, just each other's minds and aliens' I guess." Hawk shrugs.

"Guys, the bug-boy over here is trying to tell us something," Matt says, pointing a thumb at the six-eyed alien.

"His name is BUG-203, a Bipedal Unibodied Golem, acronym BUG," he chirps and clicks as Hawk translates. "He says we are on moon Bilaluna, orbiting planet Poo-ponic," Hawk continues.

Matt and I try to hold back chuckling—*BUG-203 from Planet Poo-ponic!*

The other alien introduces himself and Matt tells us, "This guy is ANT-05, ANT stands for Allied Noble Tripod".

We look at each other and then at BUG-203 and ANT-05. It occurs to us that the aliens are human-sized insectoids. *I must be in Wonderland!*

CHAPTER 10

HOLY CYBORG

ANT-05 points to a device that looks like a speaker and through it addresses everyone, "I've set my syntax generator to Earth Languages: English, so you can all understand me."

I can't believe what I'm seeing! He's a giant ant! ANT-05 is all brown and red with a shiny outer shell. His compound eyes are so huge they reflect everything around him, like mirrors. I can see myself reflected many times in his eyes! His mandibles have sharp-toothed pincers and work like scissors. I should be terrified right now, but ANT-05 seems intelligent and nice.

"I thought there were four of you when you found me. Where are the other two?" I am getting curious about these huge insects. I've always wondered what it would be like if bugs were our size. I'm a big fan of bugs. When other little girls were playing with dolls, I was asking my mom to help me collect bugs in jars. I never understood why the other girls ran away when I came near them with my jars.

"After we realized you were no threat to us, FLY-104 and RoACh-11 left for the colony to prepare everyone for your visit." ANT-05 pulls his antenna through the hairs on the inside of his foreleg like a comb and I have to force myself to stop staring at this magnified version of an ant. He's so amazing!

The cyborgs click and squeak to each other. Then BUG-203 hands each of us an oxygen mask to help us breathe as we make the journey to the colony.

We follow ANT-05, bouncing in low gravity across the bumpy lunar terrain. "Does everyone on your planet use acronyms, and numbers for names?" I ask him, as I start to make a list in my mind of these alien insect species.

"Our population consists of seven types of cyborgs that all have important jobs to ensure the survival of the colony. Our acronyms reflect our duties, and each cyborg has a number to identify them."

"What do FLY and RoACh stand for?" Matt asks.

Just then, FLY-104 zooms in from the western sky and disappears from view as he conceals himself using the black planet that Bilaluna orbits.

"Whoa, what was that?" Hawk cries, shielding his eyes and holding down his worm-dress in the rush of air. "I couldn't see him coming as he flew in front of that black dot in the sky!"

"That's what FLYs do, they are Flap Levitating Yeomen. FLY-104 is a stealth messenger for the Queen BEE. He is trained to hide his approach. He is making sure we are on our way to the colony," explains ANT-05 as he salutes FLY-104. He directs us to a high-tech moon buggy with huge balloon tires to navigate all the boulders and craters.

"What about RoACh?" Hawk asks, getting interested.

"Robot Armored Champs. RoAChs are our soldiers. They protect the colony from possible alien invaders, like you," he says, making a clicking sound that I think is laughter. "Because of their armor, they also safely transport our nectar." ANT-05 climbs into the driver seat of the buggy and we climb aboard.

"You said there are seven types. What are the other three?" I ask, overcoming my shyness. Sometimes I think I like bugs more than humans.

"I will tell you about them as we meet them," ANT-05 says, as he propels the moon buggy like a rocket over the barren moonscape. We all slam back in our seats and bump into each other as he flies over rocks and in and out of craters.

"It's so vast and empty. Was there a meteor strike or some disaster that killed all life here?" Hawk asks.

We hold on to the handlebar for dear life. ANT-05 drives the buggy 100 miles an hour over a ramp of dirt and we find ourselves airborne in the low gravity. We start to do a nosedive and ANT-05 pulls the buggy up into an air-wheelie and we land with a soft bounce on the back tires. I feel the buggy accelerate across the terrain spraying gravel everywhere, and the three of us look at each other in stunned silence. I rub my worry stone to calm myself.

ANT-05 continues navigating like nothing happened. "This is spent territory that died as we cut down trees and drew the essence from the plants," he admits.

"Why would you do that? Do you need wood to make houses?" Matt asks, bouncing up and down painfully in his seat.

"No, we live in underground burrows. We burn trees to create the energy we need to convert plant essence into nectar," says ANT-05. "We all consume nectar to survive."

"I think I see a line of trees in the distance. Is that an oasis?" I cry excitedly.

"Your vision is very good for a human with only two eyes!" says ANT-05. "Most of our population have multiple eyes, they are called ommatidia."

"Yes, I know, I've been into bugs my whole life! Err, I mean I like to study insects," I say regaining my composure. "On Earth, we have more than 800,000 species of insects and the only place that has no bugs is Antarctica." I tell them.

"Haha! ANT-arctica. You are such a joker, Celeste!" Matt laughs .

"I'm not joking, Matt." I shoot him a sideways glance.

ANT-05 adds, "You have probably never come across our species before. We are cyborgs, meaning we are organic beings with robotic parts that expand our physical abilities."

"Yippee -Ki-Yay! Super-Insects!" shouts Matt. "Like those creatures on *Star Trekkers*, 'Mute-Ants'. Get it?" He high fives Hawk as we swerve around a huge boulder and the buggy almost tips over.

"What parts of you are robotic?" I ask as I fill in the chart in my head of this new species. But my stomach rolls over and I try not to puke in my mask.

"Our brains, hearts and stomachs are organic, and the rest is robotic and mechanical," ANT-05 explains. "We evolved and made ourselves bigger, stronger and more efficient. We control our robotic body parts using telekinesis. That is how we raised you out of the crater. We advanced and developed to ensure the survival of the colony."

"That's so awesome! Why do you have a queen bee?" I wonder out loud. I know all about bees, but this is something new and fantastical.

"The Queen bee reigns as the colony's formal head of state—since it was the bees that shared their secret for making nectar from essence, which feeds the whole colony," replies ANT-05. He comes to a screeching halt in front of a line of trees, where we all tumble out, moaning.

CHAPTER 11

YOU'RE IN THE COLONY NOW

We follow ANT-05 into the oasis. The other half of the moon is a lush tropical rainforest with jungle-like vegetation and fast-moving streams. A cascading, silvery waterfall adds a cool mist to the perfect landscape. My senses are all popping right now. Tall palm trees fan out in front of us, interwoven with mangrove trees and large ferns. Underneath those, beautiful over-sized orchids and flowers grow in crazy colors, I've never even imagined. The smells, the colors, the cool wet breeze on my skin—I can't even speak right now.

"Wow," says Hawk, looking around, "this place is a giant paradise! I feel so, so tiny in here. Now I know how ants feel on Earth!"

ANT-05 stops briefly to clean his face with his forelegs. I am staring at him again when I hear my name being called from far away.

"*Celeste!*" Hawk touches my arm and I snap out of my trance.

ANT-05 sweeps a claw in front of him, "The whole moon was once like this—as was planet Poo-ponic. You can take off your masks now as the oxygen level is better here".

We cross a long bridge that spans a wide river and ANT-05 declares, "We are almost at the main entrance to the burrow."

We reach a clearing with armies of BUGs and RoAChs lined up around the entrance to a cave. FLYs zoom in and out of the opening and rub their forelegs together like I've seen houseflies do. Then a swarm of giant bees approach and zoom into the burrow. *Buzzzzzut.*

"Are those bees?" I ask, getting excited again. "They're my favorite insect of all!" I learned a lot about bees because they are like the farmers of nature. They move pollen around to germinate plants and flowers everywhere. Vegetables like broccoli and asparagus, melon and berry bushes, and even apple and willow trees would die off without bees.

"Yes," answers ANT-05. "They are Bi-winged Essence Extractors–BEEs. They collect the essence from plants that we use to make fortified nectar."

In the distance we notice some smaller beetles heading away single file, chirping a vaguely familiar marching song as they disappear into the forest. "Hi, Hole, Hidey Hole, it's off to bore we go!"

"Who are they, Humbugs?" quips Matt, who salutes them as they march away.

"They are Wood Boring Beetles or WoBBs," answers ANT-05. "They cut down trees, like your beavers, but they do it by boring holes until the flora falls."

Hawk watches the WoBBs hum as they go to work. "I think they like their jobs."

"Yes, the fermented sap on the trees keeps them happy," ANT-05 responds.

Then BUG-203 announces, "It is time to meet the Queen." I can see his brain pulsating like a beating heart.

We look at each other nervously and follow him into a grand hall lined with columns of shiny rocks like marble. The Queen BEE looks like a beautiful, human-sized, honeybee, seated on a throne of fancy, carved quartz stone.

"Whoa! How did you move all these rocks in here?" Hawk whispers to ANT-05.

"It was done by our final groups of workers—Wriggling Rock Movers or WoRMs," ANT-05 says. "The rocks were erected into columns by OAFs, the Order of ANT Freemasons, who also carved the throne for our Queen."

Matt chuckles and whispers to us, "Looks like an amazing job for a bunch of oafs."

I have to hide my nervous laughter as we approach the throne. I have a hard time meeting new people, never mind a queen. I keep my hand in my pocket so I can feel the cool smoothness of my stone for confidence. I try to avoid making eye contact as we bow down in front of the awesome Queen BEE, but I have to check out this amazing bee. She has three body parts and three pairs of legs on the middle section.

On her head are two bulbous, compound black eyes with long eyelashes and twinkly antennae with fuzzy yellow fur in between. Her small, upturned mouth smiles as her wings flutter behind her when she talks and buzzes. The beautiful Queen instructs us to tell our story.

"Hello, your Majesty. We came to Bilaluna from planet Earth through a radio wormhole," Hawk tells her. "It was an accident." He looks at me and I look down, my face burning. *Rub-Rub.*

"We are zzzso glad to meet you zzz," buzzes the Queen, putting us at ease. "We are alwayzz happy to have vizitorzz on Bilaluna. But we have been hoping for earthlingzzz to come here—ever zzzince we received mezzages from your space probe and developed the Earth language syntax generator."

I notice she speaks with a buzzing accent.

"We are surprised to meet you," Matt says. We all stare at the human-sized bee in front of us.

"We are very izzolated here on our lonely moon. You saw the devazztation on the dark side of the moon?" she buzzes.

The Queen tells of how they came to live on a dying moon. "You will be interested to know that, like you, our first colonizzers arrived on planet Poo-ponic through a wormhole from Earth zzz. Plantzz and soil alzo."

We look at each other amazed. Actual insects from Earth turned cyborg-insectoids.

"Our historians tell us that a meteorite impact opened up the wormhole and zzsucked our tiny ancestors acrozz the universe to another planet," continues the Queen. "We were transported to Poo-ponic where our kind thrived and evolved into what you zzsee before you."

"When did you leave Poo-ponic?" I ask.

"We moved to our moon through another worm-hole to ezscape when planet Poo-ponic became very zzsick." The Queen sniffs with a loud *buzzt* as we look around awkwardly and shuffle our feet. "We had to watch azz our planet died over the next hundred-thouzzand moon orbitzz. That'zz the black dot you see in the sky. I worry that the same fate izz about to befall our beautiful Bilaluna."

"Do you ever go back there?" Hawk asks.

The Queen frowns. "No, the atmozzphere is toxic, and there'zz nothing there but rock and dust zzz."

"That's so sad," I say, clenching my worry stone. I think about our beautiful planet Earth.

"Yes, our stories describe it as once even more beautiful than the unspent parts of our moon," ANT-05 adds as the Queen composes herself.

She tries to get up from her throne and two BUGs scurry over to tug on her forelegs and pull her to a standing position. "*Bzzzt!* Let go, I say, I can do thizzzz!"

The Queen takes us on a tour of the burrow. She is proud to show how all the groups work together. She leads us deeper, to an area where WoRMs and OAFs are building another wing of the burrow. They demonstrate how the vibrations of wriggling WoRMs and telekinesis are used to loosen large rocks that block tunnel construction.

As we leave the burrow, the Queen gets all abuzz.

"Zzz, what perfect timing! It'zz the ceremonial 'Waggle danzze'," she states, buzzing and fluttering excitedly.

We see many BEEs that just returned from an essence extraction excursion in the main square performing a complex dance.

"I've read about this." I say, getting excited. "They use the dance to communicate the direction and the distance of the flowers to other bees. It's the most amazing thing I've ever . . . I start to say, but burst out laughing when I turn and see Hawk and Matt trying to copy some of the dance moves—Wiggling their butts and flapping their arms like wings. I know why I like these guys—they're weirder than me.

The Queen buzzes, "You are all very clever, indeed zzz. I am sure you will enjoy the rezzt of the tour."

As the dance ends, the Queen raises her claw and ANT-05 appears out of nowhere. "Yes, my Queen?" He says.

"Take our visitorzz to the nectar generating prezzes, and both ezzence extraction and tree harvezting operationzz along the way," she orders. "Bring them back here afterwardzz for nectar sip time and a conference with the Chief and myzzelf," she buzzes, waddling back to the throne hall.

CHAPTER 12

WHAT'S THE BUZZ?

We climb aboard the moon buggy for another jolting ride through the jungle. The landscape is so green and beautiful it's hard to believe the moon is dying. ANT-05 takes a sharp right turn and almost rolls the buggy onto a narrow trail towards loud buzzing. In a clearing, we see a swarm of BEEs extracting essence from flowering plants, moving from one to another to extract as much essence as possible. It's an incredible sight to see the giant BEEs doing what bees do best. But something doesn't look natural with these robotic bees. The essence extraction process is very efficient, with very little pollen spreading from flower to flower—which most plants need to reproduce.

Matt asks the boss, ANT-51, "Why don't the BEEs spread pollen from flower to flower? I learned about pollination on my grandfather's farm."

He answers as he takes a break to groom himself "BEEs have been programmed to take all the essence without spillage or waste so that more nectar can be produced."

I tell them what I remember reading in my bee books. "You need to cross-pollinate to grow more fruit and to create seeds."

ANT-51 clicks his pincers together, "We don't need fruit as we all eat nectar, and this way produces more nectar."

Something doesn't sound right to me, but I force myself to keep quiet. Sometimes people think I'm too pushy with my ideas.

ANT-05 zooms the buggy through the jungle and takes us along another path towards crashing noises and high-pitched buzzing. I cover my sensitive ears to block the racket. There's a group of WoBBs lined up in front of a row of trees at the edge of the forest. Taking turns, they jump into holes dissecting the trees, relieving other WoBBs who are pushing out large amounts of sawdust from the holes.

ANT-05 explains, "ACEs from the Ant Corp of Engineers determine the exact number and spacing of boreholes needed to take down a tree most efficiently and safely."

The whole line of trees crashes to the ground, and a smaller group of WoBBs drill boreholes in each branch to dissect it. Within seconds, a swarm of FLYs in V formation swoop in to take the trunks and branches off to the furnaces, using levitation to carry the trees. The FLYs are directed by a group of three ANTs per tree, which ANT-05 tells us are members of AUTREs, the Ant Union of Tree Removal Experts.

Matt responds laughing, "These bugs must be part of the 'boring' clique." Hawk and I groan and roll our eyes at Matt this time.

"Boring clique. Oh brother, I think I get it." Hawk says, palming his face.

At the same time, I feel sad about the killing of all the beautiful trees I see going on here. "These trees don't stand a chance." I mutter, watching the trees fall like dominos.

ANT-05 informs us of our last destination. "We will visit the furnaces and nectar production facility at the edge of the forest."

ANT-05 chirps and squeaks out some instructions to a group of FLYs, and before I know what is happening, three of them have grabbed us by our shoulders and we're flying off to the other side of the alien jungle—Air-Bilaluna.

"Woohoo, look what I can do!" I yell at the top of my lungs, surprised by my emotions.

I hold my arms out like I'm flying and Hawk does the same. The wind whips our faces as we soar high above the lunar landscape and take in the amazing view. The hills of green and yellow fly by so fast that they look like rolling blue hills. The peaks have strange alien rock shapes dipping down to volcanic craters below. We can see the spent lands in the distance. Hawk and I get close enough that our fingertips touch and it's an amazing moment. He's real, but this feels like a dream! We are being carried by friendly, giant cyborg flies! Hawk doesn't say anything, but I can see that he is enjoying it too! We look at each other and pretend to be birds, as our toes brush the tops of the trees.

This is amazing!" screams Hawk, to be heard over a thundering waterfall. We swing by the cascade of water over a beautiful blue lagoon.

Meanwhile, Matt closes his eyes the whole way, only to vomit as we descend to the ground, narrowly missing ANT-05 who is flying behind us. "Sorry!" he chokes out as we are gently dropped onto solid ground.

"That was so cool! Can we do it again?" Hawk begs. I nod my head, unable to speak as Matt waves us away.

"I'll pass thanks," Matt says, looking apologetically at ANT-05.

ANT-05 brushes off his foreleg and combs his antennas. "Let us continue the tour."

The furnace area is a hive of activity, as another group of AUTREs direct FLYs to lower trees into the burners. ANT-05 says, "The furnaces are used to heat massive boilers to run the steam turbines that power large presses to crush essence into nectar." We enter the production hive and he continues, "The presses are organized like assembly lines managed by BUGs. They load the nectar into bins they make with a sticky thread they excrete to form a strong netting."

I exclaim, "Wow, look at them weave. It took me two months to knit a scarf last winter." It ended up with a lot of holes in it, but my dad still wore it proudly. I feel a pang when I think of my Dad and wonder if I'll ever see him again.

ANT-05 adds, "The bins are inserted into compartments inside the RoAChs who transport the nectar to the colony. RoACh shells are armored to protect against theft or damage."

"Nectar production is really important to you!" Hawk notes.

"Yes, we work together to achieve our primary goal—to produce the nectar that sustains us," replies ANT-05.

I remember my research projects on ant and bee societies. They are single-mindedly focused on the survival of the colony.

Pointing at the massive spinning cogs and wheels, ANT-05 tells us about the work of their engineers. "ACE ANT engineers are the brains of the operation. They designed the turbines used to generate the power for the energy needs of the colony."

A thought nags at the back of my brain—I hope they are smart enough to save their spent lands.

CHAPTER 13

THE GREAT RACE

"So, ANTs are large and in charge!" Matt laughs, trying to high-five ANT-05 who looks confused and moves away from him.

"ANTs first introduced telekinesis, or the ability to move objects with our minds, to our evolving species," ANT-05 informs us. "This advanced the colony so much that nobility was bestowed on the ANTs, granting us supervisor status for all operations."

"Is that how ants can carry up to 5,000 times their weight?" I ask, remembering this amazing fact.

"I once saw a tiny ant carry a cooked macaroni noodle across the kitchen floor. At first, I thought it was moving by itself," Matt exclaims, shaking his head.

"Yes," ANT-05 says, "our small ancestors used a crude form of telekinesis to carry heavy objects. we have refined it to control the movement of all objects around us. We have strong bodies and stronger minds."

"It would help my basketball game if I could do that!" Matt says with a jump and a swish noise.

"Do you use it for sports too?" Hawk inquires.

"If you mean competitions, we do not have time for that here on Bilaluna. Our one sport is to survive," he explains.

As we leave the nectar facility, ANT-05 chirps out commands to the workers. I think he is asking the

RoAChs to give us a ride back to the colony with the last load of bins.

"This is so cool! An entomologist's dream come true," I say to Hawk and Matt, as we are helped onto the backs of the RoAChs.

"An Ento what?" Matt asks.

"A bug scientist. Woohoo! I feel like Charles Darwin on the back of a giant tortoise," I holler, clinging to the back of my giant beetle. We march through a clearing, across some streams, and into the jungle. I still can't believe I am on an alien planet with no schedule to speak of—which would normally stress me out. But I feel comfortable surrounded by BUGs and my two new friends, Hawk and Matt.

"Now, *this* is fun," Matt yells, crossing a stream. He stands up on his RoACh, holding onto the ropes, pretending to whip it to go faster. "Gitty-up! Gitty-up!" he yells as his RoACh lurches out of the water and speeds up a little.

I look over at Hawk and nod toward Matt. Hawk is already standing up, urging his RoACh to run. "Okay, you guys," I say, jumping up. "Game on!" But my RoACh is slow to respond, so Hawk and Matt get a head start on me. I pat my RoACh's back and tickle her neck, begging her to speed up. She gets the message and runs like crazy. As we race over hills and valleys, weaving around trees and splashing through streams, my RoACh catches right up. "Look out, you two. coming through," I yell.

Matt, confident of his lead, yells out, "No way! Eat my dust, sucker."

Hawks shouts, "Yippee -Ki-Yay, cowboy!" as he takes the lead.

I shout, "The first one to the next stream is the winner!" I'm gaining on them as my RoACh and I bond as a team, one being to another.

We approach the next stream, and I am only one RoACh-length behind. I urge my RoACh to sprint to the finish line, and the three of us are tied when we get there. the RoAChs know that this stream is too deep to cross, so they all come to a dead stop at the edge. My RoACh is going so fast that when she stops, I go flying right over the top of her screaming, "Yippee -Ki-Oh-No!" as I land in the water with a splash.

Hawk and Matt start laughing.

"Oh man, that was a riot!" Matt chuckles.

Then Hawk notices how upset I am.

"It was all tied up. This isn't fair . . . and, and now I'm . . . all wet." I get emotional, and start to tear up. *I don't need a meltdown right now.* I cough and splash water on my face, so they don't see my tears.

Hawk jumps into the water and bends down next to me. "Are you okay, Celeste?"

I look into Hawk's worried face and it makes me laugh. I realize no one is laughing at me—my friends are helping me and laughing with me. So, I flick some water at him, but he just smiles and offers me his hand.

"Thanks again Perseus!" I wipe my tears away and take his hand. We slog back towards Matt, soaking wet and we hear a loud *Snort* coming from one of the large roaches. We burst out laughing as Matt hauls us both up the riverbank. Then all three RoAChs start snorting and flinging their heads back like they're laughing along with us. ANT-05 approaches making his clicking-laugh as he takes in the scene. Then he says something that makes us all stop laughing.

"The main square is just ahead. Who wants to taste some fresh nectar with the Queen Bee?"

Hawk, Matt and I look at each other nervously, and Hawks says, "Uhhhhhh . . . sure."

CHAPTER 14

NECTAR OF THE GODS

As we reach the burrow, BUG-203 is there to help clean us up. he offers Hawk and me dry worm-skins to wear. Then he ushers us into the great hall where the Queen and Chief are waiting for us.

Matt looks sideways at me and Hawk. "Look at you two, you really are the 'worm-ones'! Why didn't I bring a camera?" He says, with a snicker.

"Welcome back. Did you enjoy the tour zzz?" Buzzes the Queen happily.

"Yes, Your Majesty, very much. This half of the planet is very beautiful!" Hawk offers, not mentioning the spent lands.

"I want you to meet our ANT Chief. He'zz our top engineer. Chief, theezze are the exceptional young people I wazz telling you about. Meet Hawk, Matt, and Celeste from Planet Earth zzz. It'zz a miracle, I tell you, zzimply a miracle!" says the Queen, wiping tears from her many eyes with a cloth.

"I, for one, am not happy about aliens on our moon. Especially, human aliens!" He snaps, glaring at us.

"Pleazze Chief zzz! You said you would keep an open mind about thizz. Hawk, Matt, and Celeste want to help us with our 'moon' crisizz! Izzn't that right?"

"Uhhh, yes Ma'am," Hawk says for all of us. I can't even speak.

"Which one of you wants to explain this?" Chief demands, showing us a piece of folded paper. We look at one another and shrug. Chief awkwardly unfolds the paper with his claws and reads: "The insect apocalypse and why humans are driving the extinction of all insect-kind. Humans are trying to kill insects as quickly and efficiently as possible; by poisoning, electrocuting and trapping them." He looks at us with a scowl while the Queen covers her mouth with a tissue.

I slowly raise my hand and everyone looks at me in surprise. "Um that's notes for my science paper. It must have fallen out of my pocket in the moon buggy."

"What is the meaning of this?" Bursts Chief, still reading through the outline of my research project.

"I, I . . . was writing my paper on the advantages of having insects in our society and how people should stop trying to kill them," I say in a sad voice, knowing how bad it sounds.

"You mean people on Earth use chemicals to kill insects?" Chief mutters in shock. "According to this, humans kill 75% of insects every Earth year with insectigone."

"My paper was supposed to make people see how important insects are to our ecosystem. How they pollinate plants and are an important part of the food chain. At the end I say that people must stop using pesticides."

"Okay Chief. Let'zz put all that behind uzz and focus on the problem at hand. Thezze young people are not the ones killing antz or beez! zzz They want to help." The Queen pats Chief on the shoulder and leads him over to a sitting area and indicates we should follow. The Chief turns away from us angrily. "We need help to save our dying moon. But how can we trust you not to poison us or set a trap to kill us?" He frowns at us.

"I'm really sorry that some humans don't treat insects very well, and we need to do better. But it's not all humans. There are many humans who love insects and want to learn about them and protect them. Please let us try to help you."

He looks up at me sharply. "I can't blame you for the mistakes of all humanity—but I hope you realise that insects are people too. *Grunt*! We are intelligent, caring and sensitive creatures." He makes a trilling sound and we look away.

"Now then, BUG-203 can you bring the nectar trolley zzz? Pleazze pour nectar for everyone," the Queen instructs.

Hawk, Matt, and I look into our cups nervously.

"You try it, Hawk," says Matt.

"No, you go first!" Hawk says, turning red.

"No, I went first last time," argues Matt.

I grab my cup and drink down the entire thing. Hawk and Matt look at me with their mouths hanging open and wait for my reaction. Wiping my mouth on my worm-dress, I let out a big *Buuuurrrpppp!* "Excuse me," I say, with a giggle.

Hawk and Matt are shocked, but they grab their cups and slurp down the golden liquid.

"This is so delicious," Hawk exclaims, surprised that it tastes so good. "It's like, better than cola and milk."

We all look at each other and crack up laughing.

"I've never tasted anything so sweet and yummy!" I say, rubbing my tummy and giggling again.

"One, two, three, four. I declare a thumb war!" Hawk says, looking at Matt.

"You're on, Hawk, you know I always beat you," Matt crows.

They grab hands and wrestle with their thumbs until the Queen orders them to stop and be serious.

"Sorry, your Majesty. But I suddenly feel very strong and full of energy," Hawk says.

"That's the nectar. Isn't it marvelouzz!" buzzes the Queen BEE, fluttering behind her wings.

"What can you tell us about Earth's environmental protections?" asks Chief, gulping his nectar.

Hawk tells us about Mr. Longsnout's environmental science class and what they learned about hydroelectric power. "What if you use the power from waterfalls and rivers instead of burning trees to power the turbines? You could have all the clean energy you need," he suggests.

Chief wipes his eyes and considers this possibility. We can see his anxiety going up again as he holds his large triangular head in his foreclaws.

Matt, who spent summers on the farm with his grandfather, offers, "It would help the spent land if you could irrigate it with water from the nearby river."

The chief throws his forelimbs up in the air and chirps angrily, as Matt continues, "And, my Grandpoppa told me that it's important to let the bees cross-pollinate flowers while they are collecting nectar and pollen. That way you produce more plants, fruit and the seeds to regrow your fields of flowers and trees."

Chief starts clicking and grunting to the Queen as she ignores him.

I think about my mother's composting projects and even though they were very stinky I share them, "Maybe it would help to spread the plant waste or compost, like sawdust and droppings, on the dead land to make it more fertile and able to grow things again," I say tucking my hair behind my ear, and not making eye contact with anyone. *Rub-Rub on my smooth, cool stone.*

"We learned in school that you should always replant the trees you cut down to have clean air and healthy forests. It'll help to recover the spent part of the moon," Hawk adds, sounding like Mr. Longsnout.

Sniffing and snorting the Chief snaps, "Of course we've tried to replant trees, and it doesn't work. We have a very efficient system in place to make enough nectar for all of Bilaluna. We wouldn't want to risk hunger and starvation of the masses," says the Chief, clicking to himself and compulsively cleaning his antenna. "Besides the WoBBs would be jobless. No, I'm afraid the AUTREs will never agree," he grunts, pacing the floor, pulling and tearing at his antennas.

"Pleazze Chief, I think thezze ideazz are worthy," says the Queen between sips of nectar. "We have to do zzzomething or risk the same fate as Poo-ponic." She sniffs loudly and wipes her eyes again.

"The WoBBs could still bore holes in fallen branches to help them decompose faster and make more fertile soil," I tell him what I know about our Earth beetles.

"I need to meet with the ACEs, AUTREs, and OAFs to see if we can make these changes without too much cyborg suffering," says Chief. "But they will not like it." He dashes from the hall without another word.

"We have a question for you too," Hawk says to the Queen. "Can you help us get back to Planet Earth?"

The Queen looks at us in surprise. "We azzumed you would zztay here on Bilaluna zzz. Going back through a wormhole izz very dangerouzzz," she buzzes sadly, shaking her head.

"But we have to go home. Our families will worry if we're not home in time for dinner," Hawk says.

We all agree that we will have to risk the trip back through the wormhole to get home. I miss my parents, and my room, and my books, and . . .

CHAPTER 15

HOW DO YOU LIKE YOUR EGGS?

ater that day, Hawk, Matt, and I try to take our minds off getting back to Earth by playing a game with some of the baby BUGs in the burrow. "Okay," yells Matt, "This is what we're going to do. We three go and hide and you guys count to twenty." He shows them his ten fingers two times. "And then come find us!" The baby BUGs shriek and then chirp and click happily as we run off to find a good hiding spot.

"This way," Hawk whispers, going left towards a hidden tunnel. Luckily, they gave Hawk and I our own clean clothes back because it's cold down here.

"It looks awfully dark down there," I say, slowing down. "Let's stay around here where it's brighter."

"We'll be too easy to find," Hawk says, reaching to take my hand. When I hesitate, he looks at me and hooks his arm through my arm. I reach out and hook my other arm through Matt's arm. I look at Hawk with a shy smile. I think he understands that I have a hard time with physical contact.

"Okay, let's go," I say feeling more confident with my friends around me. I still can't believe that I have two best friends and they're both boys! How did this happen? Just last week I had no friends and I was terrified to even talk to a boy.

We go down deeper and deeper into the tunnel to look for someplace to hide. Matt holds his nose and coughs. "What is that gross smell?"

Despite the horrible stench, we travel a little further down to investigate.

As the odor gets almost unbearable, we notice piles of slimy white stuff that looks like tiny, drippy eggs.

"What is that stuff?" Hawk asks with his shirt covering his nose.

I tell them, "It looks like rotting insect eggs, like the ones in my ant farm at home."

As the smell of decomposing eggs starts to overcome us, Matt yells, "Let's get out of here, I can't breathe!"

We stumble over our feet trying to get away from the stank. Rushing out of the tunnel we are swarmed by baby BUGs clicking and chirping excitedly as they pick us up and carry us the rest of the way out.

That night, I need some quiet time to gather my thoughts and go over the events of the day. I find a warm, quiet corner in the burrow. I still feel badly about the research paper, but I can't shake the feeling that I am missing something. I think about the eggs in the tunnel as I drowse into a light sleep. I wake to find myself back in the dark tunnel, all alone. *Did I sleepwalk or something? Where are Hawk and Matt?* I keep walking because I need to get out of here. I cover my nose and step over the piles of rotting eggs. I am drawn towards a chamber at the far end of the tunnel. There's a large insectoid hunched over in the corner. I think it's ANT-05, and feel a sense of relief. *He'll help me.* I approach and whisper "ANT-05 can you . . . " he turns to look at me, and I see it's not ANT-05—it's a really old ANT. He uncurls himself to monstrous proportions and stares down at me. Spikey grey hairs cover his exoskeleton and his crooked legs creak as they straighten out. "How does it feel to be the tiny ones on OUR planet?" he grins at me and I slowly back away.

"Who, who are you?" I stammer.

"I am ANT. The first of my kind, so I have no number. I was the lab insect used for testing before cyborg creation. I have been around a long time and I know many things."

"Why are you here, in the stinky, rotting egg tunnel?" I ask in a tiny voice, ready to bolt.

"I watch over our eggs, because they are important," he answers.

"Why are there so many?" I ask, looking around at all the gooey piles everywhere.

"You will understand when you see the big picture. But to see, you must look," he says as he disappears into a mist in the burrow.

"ANT, wait I don't understand," I call out. It's useless, he's gone. "ANT! ANT!" I wake up, sweaty in my warm corner and put my wrist to my mouth to stop myself from crying out. Was it a dream? I sit up on my mat and hug my knees and rock back and forth. *What did he mean? The eggs are important and look at the big picture.*

I close my eyes because my brain starts showing me pictures in fast motion—like a movie. Pictures are faster than words, so I get a 360-degree view of my bug books, the woods at home and moon Bilaluna. It strikes me that, other than cyborg super-insects there are no small insects on the moon—not in the jungle or the trees or anywhere! As soon as I see Hawk and Matt, I ask them if they had seen any small insects on Bilaluna. They agree that they must have wiped out all of the original small insect species. But why?

***

Chief returns to meets us in the great hall. "We met and I convinced the others that your ideas are helpful, and you are not trying to make insects needlessly suffer," he informs us. "We are working to convert the steam turbines from running on the energy of burning trees to water turbine generators. The WoRMs are digging ditches for irrigation of the spent lands."

The Queen nods and buzzes, "The BEEzz have been reprogrammed to begin crozz-pollination to expand zzeed production for replanting. We are hopeful that we can have at leazzt 10% of spent land back by the next growing zycle zzz. This is very encouraging!" she cries. "I knew there was a reazzon for your vizzit to Bilaluna zzz."

I have to tell the Queen what we discovered during our hide-and-seek game. "When we were playing with the baby BUGs, we found a very smelly tunnel that seemed to have lots of rotting eggs."

The Queen gets upset, and fans herself, her antennae sagging, she replies, "You zzhould not have gone down there. That izz one of the zzacred tunnelzz, where we bury our unused eggz."

"Unused eggs?" I say, confused.

"Yezz," says the Queen. "We only fertilizze enough eggz for the cyborg insectz needed to maintain our colony. There are many millionz of eggs that are unnecezzary," she says wiping at her eyes.

"Is that why you don't have any small insects on Bilaluna?" Hawk asks.

"Yezz," says the Queen. "We can't create that many cyborgz, so we just don't fertilizze them. We bury the eggz deep in the tunnel out of rezpect."

My brain kicks into overdrive again, and I see all my insect knowledge in front of me like a video. An important part of the solution comes to me in an instant. Like a puzzle piece falling into place with a click. I blurt out, "But if there were small insects in the forest, they would regenerate soil from the dying plants. I read that ants alone add almost half a centimeter of soil to the surface of the Earth every year, and wood-boring beetles add even more." I have an encyclopedia of information in my brain to share.

The Queen excitedly declares, "Meaning our forestzz would be healthier if we fertilizze all the eggz and breed millionz of small insectz?"

"Yes," I continue, "and worms dig up 18 tons of soil per acre every year."

"Why didn't we think of that?" the Queen exclaims. "Celeste, you are more brilliant than the starzz in the cosmozz you were named for."

"Yah Celeste, it's cool that you know so much about insects," says Hawk, high fiving me.

I blush, but I feel proud. I never imagined that all my obsessing about insects could be so helpful. I go through phases where I just consume information on a certain topic. And even though it's weird sometimes, it's nice to know I can make a difference, at least in this world.

Chief notes, "Our tiny insect ancestors are more important than we thought."

"Yes. That's what ANT said," I tell them.

"Which ANT?" asks ANT-05.

"Just ANT. The first, really old one. He helped me figure out that the small insects were important." I look around at all the confused faces.

"ANT is no longer with us. He died many moons ago," says ANT-05 with a sad click.

"Oh . . . I guess it was a dream," I say. *It seemed so real.* I feel the hair on the back of my neck rise up. *Did I talk to a ghost?*

"Well, that settlezz it," declares the Queen, "from now on we fertilizze all our eggzz and share our moon with our small anceztorz.

CHAPTER 16

A ROCKIN' EXTRAVAGANZZA

After celebrating with lots of yummy nectar, ANT-05 takes us on another tour of Bilaluna in the moon buggy. We watch as the cyborg WoRMs tunnel through the hardened terrain towards the river. The water will flood the spent lands and prepare it for replanting. The giant BEEs in the fields, serious in their work, caress each flower as they extract the essence, leaving behind a trail of pollen in their wake. ANT-05 takes us by the furnaces to view the engineers building a dam across the river to power the turbines and generators. We can't believe how quickly the insects have put our advice into action. The way they work, they'll have clean energy and new plants growing in no time.

Back at the burrow, Hawk pleads with the Queen, "Now that we helped you save your moon, can you help us get home?"

"Yez Hawk, although we would love it if you could stay zzz," replies the Queen. "We can bring you back to the crater where we found you. I believe you'll find the wormhole is zztill there," she buzzes.

ANT-05 adds, "We'll have our BUGs spin cocoons over old WoRM skins to create a protective egg for you to travel safely through the wormhole."

"I will give you my zpecial cocktail of nectar and

BEE venom that will put you in suzpended animation, zzz. Your journey will be painlezz and over before you know it," declares the Queen. "However, before you go, we have an extravaganzza planned in your honor."

As soon as the Queen says extravaganza, there is a great buzzing outside the burrow.

We head outside and there are hundreds of BEEs and FLYs hovering in the sky. The buzzing sounds are so loud I cover my ears, and the insects darken the sky.

"Pleazze enjoy this airshow as a token of our apprezziation," calls the Queen from her throne in front of the square. She raises her claw to begin the celebration.

Swarms of BEEs and FLYs buzz by at rapid speeds, showing off what they can do. Flying over and under each other, doing loop-de-loops, and weaving in and out of each other's lanes. FLYs then BEEs approach slowly and hover. each group creates a letter above us. First FLYs in T formation, then BEEs forming an H, then FLYs and BEEs alternating the letters --- A --- N --- K --- Y --- O --- U. Spelling THANK YOU! Finally, a line of FLYs come in low, right over us holding torches that light up in different colors. They rise and fall spreading outward in all directions like fireworks.

We jump up and down and clap as the Queen beams at us. She nods at another group of BEEs to indicate they're up next. The BEEs gather together in a swarm to prepare for their performance. The BEEs at the center of the group turn slightly to reflect the light off their wings and make a dark heart-shaped spot. The BEEs next to them turn one after another all the way to the outside, making a heart-shaped ripple that moves outwards like a Mexican wave. Then the ripple moves back towards the center. They repeat this over and over, so it looks like a beating heart of bees.

"Look!" Matt cries, pointing "They're doing the wave."

"This is called shimmering," the Queen tells us "We beezz use it for important moments. zzz They're sending you a mezzage zzz."

We turn around because it sounds like a thunderstorm approaching. It's the sound of hundreds of marching cyborg RoAChs, stomping in formation. They parade passed us and WoBBs jump from one to another, like water jumping from fountain to fountain. The WoBBs drop sawdust like confetti as they fly. At the same time, BUGs file two by two around the perimeter of the square with WoRMs over their shoulders, wriggling like ribbons waving in the wind.

We stare at each other and bend over laughing as we watch with delight.

The parading roaches march in a timed beat and a rhythm emerges. A stomp-stomp clap and pause beat. I know this beat, so I look at Hawk and stomp my feet then clap. He joins in: *Stomp-Stomp Clap!* I can't remember the song but looking at the Queen reminds me of it. I poke Matt; *Stomp-Stomp Clap!* He nods and does it too. *Stomp-Stomp Clap!* The marching RoAChs are stomping and clapping to the same beat. *Stomp-Stomp Clap! Stomp-Stomp Clap!* We notice the Queen stomping her feet from atop her perch on the throne. She encourages all the rest who are watching to join in this amazing moment of human and insect unity. *Stomp-Stomp Clap!* The rhythm gets louder and builds as the cyborg groups join in the thunderous anthem.

The Queen stands and raises her claw as we follow the parade and stomp our way to the center of the square. She calls out an order to her sentry BEEs, who bend a knee.

"Climb aboard zzz!" the Queen shouts. "The marching dizzplay izz much better seen from above."

We climb on the fuzzy backs of the sentries and Matt clings on for dear life as the sentries rise up and hover above the square. *Stomp-Stomp Clap!* It's an amazing view of this giant insect celebration! The spectator cyborgs stomp and clap while the RoAChs show off their marching abilities. They march in alternating lines, weaving in and out to form shapes of spinning pinwheels and spirals. Finally, they form a circle then shift around until they've formed the words BON VOYAGE FRIENDS.

Shocked and astonished, we almost fall off our BEE carriers! We all cheer and wave as the Queen flies up to lead us around the square like a buzzing helicopter. My tears overflow as I realize we helped to save their beautiful moon. She heads down to the ground in the middle of the square, where Chief, ANT-05, BUG-203, FLY-104, RoACh-11 and the baby BUGs are assembled to see us off.

The Chief approaches us. "Thank you for helping us to see things differently and save our moon. We are already breeding several hundred thousand small insects to work the soil on our moon," he adds while bowing, "We have decided to send a team of scientists and small insects to our old planet to assess the damage and begin soil rejuvenation there, if possible."

"That's amazing!" I reply, getting choked up again.

"You have given uz hope where there wazzz none, and for that, we are eternally grateful zzz," The Queen buzzes with tears in her eyes.

"I can't believe how quickly you got all this done!" Hawk says with a shake of his head.

"Well, we are busy BEEzzz!" the Queen beams proudly.

CHAPTER 17

THIS IS HAWK—TO TELL YOU HOW IT ENDS

awk here taking over from Celeste. When we arrive at the wormhole, the Queen announces, "We have bestowed one of you with a zspecial gift that we hope zstill workz in Earth'z higher gravity zzz. Also, we have named the new wing of the colony for zzmall inzect breeding, CHuM, for Celeste, Hawk and Matt, our new chumzz." She bows to us buzzing softly.

Matt, Celeste and I bow to the Queen BEE then do our space-club handshake. We give the Queen and ANT-05 a hug, and no one minds when Celeste doesn't join in. We laugh as we watch Celeste awkwardly try to do an elbow bump with the Queen BEE. Sharing this experience with Matt and Celeste has created like a special bond between us—we're friends, and good friends accept you for who you are.

The Queen offers us her sweet nectar to drink, and we climb into our cocoon spacecraft for the journey back through the wormhole. Matt and I are not as worried as the first time, so I tell Celeste everything will be okay.

"Safe travelzz CHuMz!" says the Queen, doing a little waggle dance and wiping her teary eyes.

"Goodbye!" we say together, waving to our cyborg friends. The egg closes over us, and we're sucked into the wormhole at light-speed. We spin backward through the time-space abyss like a pinball machine on overdrive. The wormhole shrinks and expands, tilts and straightens as cool flames lick at our cocoon and we quickly fall into a nectar-induced sleep as the pressure builds inside our protective shell.

Bang, Bang, Bang! I wake up to a pounding on the door.

"Huh, what?" I say groggily, looking around at the carnage in the garage. My garage! That means we made it back. alive! I've never been so happy to see this dirty old, haunted garage.

"Celeste, Matt! Wake up! We made it home!" I say, rousing them from the wrecked egg-craft.

"Are we alive?" asks Matt, squeezing my arm, to make sure we're not dreaming.

"I think so!" Celeste says, stumbling around on pieces of old WoRM skins.

We help each other into 'Mission Control' and fall onto the couch. "Wow! Did we really just . . ." I am interrupted by the pounding on the door!

Bang, Bang, Bang!

"Celeste are you in there?" a muffled and nervous voice cries from outside.

BANG!
BANG!

"That must be your parents coming to pick you up. Time stands still here on Earth when we travel through the wormhole," I say as I tuck a strand of Celeste's wild red hair behind her ear and look deep into her eyes. "Yes, that's my dad," Celeste says, blushing and quickly looking away. She jumps up and shakes her head as if to clear it before grabbing her stuff and running for the door. She shouts, "I'll be right there, Dad!" But before opening it, she tells us, "This is the best space club ever!"

When she opens the door, she is so excited to see her dad again, she does something that surprises everyone. She throws her arms around his neck in a big hug. "Hi, Dad! Let's go home." Then she says, "Can you show me those maps of the Milky Way again?"

AUTHOR'S NOTE

A FRIEND WITH ASPERGER'S

Young people who have Asperger syndrome* usually have high intelligence, but they tend to play, learn, speak, and act a little differently from others. If you meet a new friend with Asperger's they may do some of these things:

- Obsess over a single interest.
- Crave repetition and routine (don't respond well to change).
- Miss social cues in play and conversation.
- Not make eye contact with friends and adults.
- Tend to take things too literally.
- May not like to be touched or may have unusual reactions to noises, smells, or tastes.

---

* *Asperger syndrome is a form of autism.*

GLOSSARY OF SPACE AND SCIENCE TERMS

ACE: Ant Corp of Engineers (ANTs that supervise construction).

Acronym: A word made from letters that are the first letters of other words.

ANT: Allied Noble Tripod (supervisor, diplomat).

Asperger Syndrome: is a developmental disorder where people have difficulties in social interactions and display obsessive behavior. It is on the Autism spectrum.

Astronomer: A scientist who studies planets and the sun in our solar system, as well as other stars, galaxies, and the universe.

Atmosphere: Gases surrounding a star or planet held in place by gravity.

AUTRE: ANT Union of Tree Removal Experts (ANTs that direct tree cutting and removal).

BEE: Bi-winged Essence Extractor (nectar gatherer).

BUG: Bipedal Unibodied Golem (assistant, bin-spinner).

Constellation: A group of stars that form an imaginary outline or pattern, typically representing an animal, mythological god, person or creature, or other.

Copernicus, Nicolaus: A 15th-century astronomer who first proposed the earth and other planets revolved around the sun.

Cosmologist: A scientist who studies the universe.

Cyborg: A being whose physical abilities are extended beyond normal limitations by mechanical elements built into the body.

Darwin, Charles: A 17th century, English naturalist, geologist and entomologist known for his theory of evolution.

E=mc²: Refers to the equation: energy (E) equals mass (m) times the speed of light (c) squared (multiplied by itself). It shows that energy and mass are different forms of the same thing.

Einstein, Albert: A 19-20th century theoretical physicist who developed the theory of relativity.

Electromagnetic field: A combination of invisible electric and magnetic force fields.

Entomologist: A Scientist who studies insects.

ESP: Extra Sensory Perception. The ability to read each other's thoughts.

FLY: Flap Levitating Yeoman (messenger, gopher, tree transporter).

Force-field: A barrier made up of energy, plasma or particles to protect a person, area or object from attacks.

Gravitational field (gravity): The force by which a planet or moon draws objects toward its center. Generally, the larger a planet or moon, the more gravity it exerts.

Hawking, Stephen: A 20-21st century cosmologist and theoretical physicist known for his work with black holes and relativity theory.

Insectoids: A creature or object that shares a similar body or traits with common Earth insects. Another term for cyborg insects.

Intergalactic: A term meaning between galaxies.

Irrigation: What farmers do to add water to their fields when there is not enough rain.

Levitation: The raising or lifting of a person or thing using telekinesis.

Light pollution: When surrounding lights make it difficult to see stars and planets in the night sky.

Light-speed: The speed at which light travels (about 1.08 billion km per hour).

Lunar: Related to a moon, based on the French word for moon – lune.

Mandibles: A pair of mouthparts (or jaws) of an insect designed for holding or biting food, materials.

Meteor: A piece of rock or other matter from space that produces bright light as it travels through a planet's atmosphere or the gases that surround the planet.

Meteorite: A meteor that doesn't burn up in the atmosphere and strikes a planet or moon.

Meteor shower: A large number of meteors seen in the same area of space over a short time-period.

Milky Way: A hazy band of light seen in the night sky formed from stars of earth's galaxy that are so far away they cannot be individually identified by the naked eye.

OAF: Order of ANT Freemasons (ANTs that supervise building construction).

Ommatidia: A cluster of small eyes that make up a larger insect eye.

Orbit: A path travelled around an object, such as a planet.

Pincer: The part of an insect that enables it to carry loads, to defend against other creatures, or to attack prey. For ants, pincers are part of the mandibles.

Pollination: When pollen from one flowering plant is transferred to another (also cross pollination). Pollen is often carried by flying insects such as bees. This process is important for producing seeds to generate new plants.

Portal: A gateway to another world of the past, present, or future.

Possi: A large group of beetles.

RoACh: Robot Armored Champ (defensive soldier, nectar transporter).

Sensory overload: The brain is unable to process things you see, hear, smell, taste, or touch all at once.

Supernova: Is the explosion of a star. It makes the star look super bright and sometimes leaves behind a blackhole.

Syntax generator: A machine that translates insect language and generates the basic sounds of different languages.

Telekinesis: The ability to move objects at a distance by mental power.

Theory of Relativity: A scientific explanation about how space relates to time.

Turbine: An engine that turns fluid or gas movement into energy, like a waterwheel or a windmill.

WoBB: Wood-Boring Beetle (tree cutter)

WoRM: Wriggling Rock Mover (tunneller, burrower).

Wormhole: A tunnel connecting points in space-time in such a way that the trip between the points through the wormhole takes much less time than the trip through normal space.

Worry Stone: Like a fidget spinner or other calming device to help people to self-soothe when they feel anxious. It's a comfort habit.

ACKNOWLEDGMENTS

I would like to thank the people who helped to make this project possible. Always first and foremost, my supportive and talented husband, Terry. He always had the solution to plot holes and stumbling blocks. He has also written a young adult backstory to this book entitled *The Rise and Fall of Antocracy*, which will be released soon. Many thanks to my talented and tireless editors, who found the plot holes: Isabelle Schumacher and Talya Pardo. A special thank you to Elisabeth Allen for her invaluable advice and input to Celeste's Asperger's Syndrome, her character traits and reactions in the story. Thanks to my kids, who were very enthusiastic about this endeavor from the beginning. I love you: Justin, Sophie and Kelly.

ABOUT THE AUTHOR

Ann Birdgenaw is a librarian in an elementary school and always wanted to write a book of her own. She was inspired to write the stories in this series by a strange beeping coming from a box in her garage. When COVID-19 hit Canada and everyone was in quarantine or lock down, she had lots of time to imagine being sucked through a wormhole to other planets and what wonderful things she might find there.

Ann lives in Montreal, Quebec, Canada with her family and two morkies: Bilbo and Sheba.

Visit Ann at:
https://www.goodreads.com/author/show/21269547.Ann_Birdgenaw
https://www.facebook.com/Author-Ann-Birdgenaw-109480387962145/?ref=pages_you_manage

@abirdgenaw on Twitter
@annbirdbooks on Instagram

ABOUT THE ILLUSTRATOR

E.M. Roberts is an avid intellectual property creator and illustrator. He graduated from Dawson College, Illustration and Design program in Montreal, Quebec. Among his interests are character design, futuristic aesthetic(s) and sparkling water. He lives in Montreal with his wife and two children.

Visit Ellis at:
https://www.behance.net/EllisRoberts

**Stay Tuned for *Ka'Azula*, Book 3 in the
Black Hole Radio Series!**

Stay tuned for another fantastic episode of *Black Hole Radio – Ka'Azula!*

Fifth-graders Hawk, Matt and Celeste have been given special gifts by the amazing aliens they've met so far on their intergalactic adventures. ESP and telekinesis come in handy when they are transported to the racist planet, Ka'Azula, where only blue skin is accepted. They have an action-packed adventure in a matrix-type video game with azulanimals and azulizards and a tricky escape room finale. With help from a sweet, red-skinned alien named Teal, they prove that what counts is not outside skin color but what's on the inside. But does Matt now understand what his father's family has to endure on Planet Earth?

"Friendship, peace, and acceptance are the themes in *Black Hole Radio*. Even if it doesn't yet apply to alien races in 'real-life' it is still something everyone should strive for in their lives. In a sense, the author wants her readers to apply the same beliefs in love, peace, and friendship that Hawk, Matt, and Celeste share."
—Entrada Book Review